Treasure Island

ROBERT LOUIS STEVENSON

STERLING CHILDREN'S BOOKS
New York

STERLING CHILDREN'S BOOKS
New York

An Imprint of Sterling Publishing
387 Park Avenue South
New York, NY 10016

"The Treasure Map"
Published 2006 by Sterling Publishing, Co.
Illustrations © 2006 by Sally Wern Comport
"Off to the Sea"
Published 2006 by Sterling Publishing, Co.
Illustrations © 2006 by Sally Wern Comport
"On the Island"
© 2007 by Sterling Publishing Co., Inc.
Illustrations © 2007 by Sally Wern Comport
"Pirate Attack"
© 2007 by Sterling Publishing Co., Inc.
Illustrations © 2007 by Sally Wern Comport
"Adventure at Sea"
© 2010 by Sterling Publishing Co., Inc.
Illustrations © 2010 by Sally Wern Comport
"A Pirate Adventure"
© 2010 by Sterling Publishing Co., Inc.
Illustrations © 2010 by Sally Wern Comport

ISBN 978-1-4549-0585-1 (hardcover)
ISBN 978-1-4549-0586-8 (paperback)

Distributed in Canada by Sterling Publishing
^c/o Canadian Manda Group, 165 Dufferin Street
Toronto, Ontario, Canada M6K 3H6
Distributed in the United Kingdom by GMC Distribution Services
Castle Place, 166 High Street, Lewes, East Sussex, England BN7 1XU
Distributed in Australia by Capricorn Link (Australia) Pty. Ltd.
P.O. Box 704, Windsor, NSW 2756, Australia

For information about custom editions, special sales, and premium and corporate purchases,
please contact Sterling Special Sales at 800-805-5489 or specialsales@sterlingpublishing.com.

Manufactured in China
Lot #:
2   4   6   8   10   9   7   5   3   1
06/13

www.sterlingpublishing.com/kids

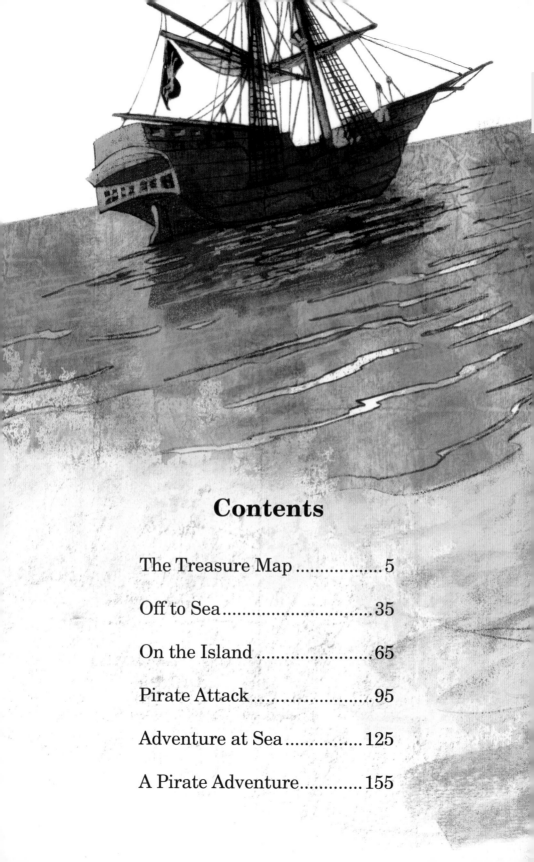

Contents

CHAPTER ONE

The Treasure Map

A young boy stood
in front of a door.
He put up his hand.
He wanted to knock,
but he was scared.
He put down his hand.
He was not sure
what he should do.

Squire Trelawney
was behind the door.
He was an important man.
Would he have time
to see a little boy
with a big story?

The boy thought about it.
He made up his mind.
The squire would want
to hear the story.

The boy knocked.

"Come in," a voice said.

The boy took a deep breath.

He opened the door.

The squire sat in a room
filled with many books.
Doctor Livesey
sat across from him.

"Who might you be?"
the squire asked the boy.
"Jim Hawkins," the boy said.
His voice was very tiny.

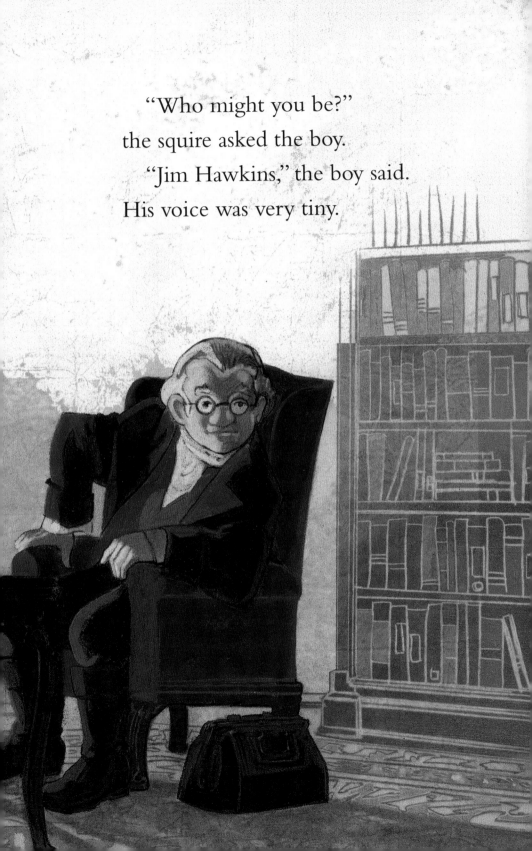

"Speak up, Jim,"
said the squire.
"Don't be scared,"
said the doctor.

Jim talked louder.

"Sirs," he said,
"I have a story to tell you."

"Tell us, my boy!"
said the squire.

"We are listening,"
the doctor said.
Jim took a deep breath.
His story came out
in one big rush.

"My family owns an inn.
Today pirates broke into it.
I was at the front desk.
I hid behind the desk.

"We had money on the desk,
but the pirates did not want it.
They wanted something else . . .

. . . something out of
the captain's sea chest!

"The captain was a sailor.
He had been staying at the inn.
He liked to sing songs
and tell stories about pirates.

"One day, he went away.
He left the chest behind.

"The pirates opened the chest.
They took everything out.
One pirate said they were
looking for a packet.
They could not find it.
They got angry.
They made a lot of noise.
Then they left."

"Where could the packet be?"
the squire asked.
Jim smiled and said,
    "Here it is, sirs!"
He pulled it out
of his pocket.

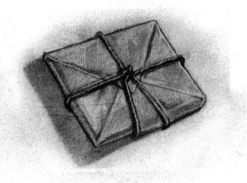

"*You* have it?" asked the doctor.

"Yes," Jim said.

"Before the pirates came,
I saw it by the chest.
I wanted to give it
to the captain,
but he never came back.
I believe the squire
might be able to help."

"Let's see," said the doctor.
Jim gave him the packet.
The doctor cut it open.
Inside was a
sheet of paper.
It had a
drawing on it.
  "It's a map!"
the squire said.

"The pirates wanted it,"
said the doctor. "It must
be important!"
 "It is," the squire said.
"It's a treasure map!"

Jim pointed to
a large X on the map.
 "What is this?" he asked.
 "That, my boy,"
said the doctor,
"is where the treasure is!"

The squire stood up.
He began to walk
around and around.

"This is exciting!"
he said. "Pirates' treasure.
I have always wanted
to find pirates' treasure!"

"We *could* go find it," the doctor said.
"I will buy a ship!" said the squire.

Jim watched the men
make their plans
to hunt for the treasure.
He wished he could go, too!

Jim didn't want to leave,
but he knew it was time
to go back to the inn.
He started to walk away.

"Where are you going?"
the squire asked Jim.

"Back to the inn," said Jim.

"Please wait," the squire said.
"We need a cabin boy
to work on the ship."

"Will you do it, Jim?"
asked the doctor.

"We will split the
treasure with you."
How Jim wanted to go—
but what about the inn?
They needed him there.

Jim could just see
all the gold and silver.
The money would be
a big help to his family . . .

. . . and Jim had always wanted
to go to sea.
He had always dreamed
of adventure.

"I will go home and see
if I can go," said Jim.
"I am sure it will be all right."
"My boy," the squire said,
"your adventures are beginning!"

CHAPTER TWO

Off to Sea

Jim Hawkins stood
on the ship's deck.
It was about to sail.
It was headed
for Treasure Island!
Pirates had buried
treasure there.
Jim and his friends
hoped to find it
and bring it back.

The anchor came out
of the deep, blue water.
Wind filled the sails.
  "We're off!" cried Jim.

The ship's captain saw Jim.

"You, on deck," he said.

"Don't just stand there.

Go help the cook fix dinner."

Jim hurried away.

The cook's name was
Long John Silver.
Long John had a wooden leg.
He walked with a crutch.

"Come in, Jim," said Long John.

"Meet Captain Flint."

Jim looked around.

"Where is he?" Jim asked.

"I don't see anyone."

Long John pulled
a sheet off a cage.
Inside was a parrot.
"Hello! Hello!"
squawked the parrot.

"I named him after
a famous pirate,"
Long John said.
Jim let out a gasp.
Pirates scared him!

"Don't you worry,"
Long John said.
"There are no pirates
on this ship, Jim."
Jim felt much better.
Long John was his friend.
Jim could trust him.

The days passed quickly.
Jim worked very hard.
The work made Jim hungry.
Luckily, there was plenty
of food on the ship.
There was even a whole
barrel of apples to pick from.

One day, Jim reached
into the barrel.
It was almost empty.
Just a few apples were
still at the bottom.
Jim climbed inside
to get one of them.

It was dark
inside the barrel.
Jim was tired.
He closed his eyes.
He would rest
for just a minute.

Jim dozed off.

Suddenly, he was jolted awake.

Someone was sitting next to the barrel.

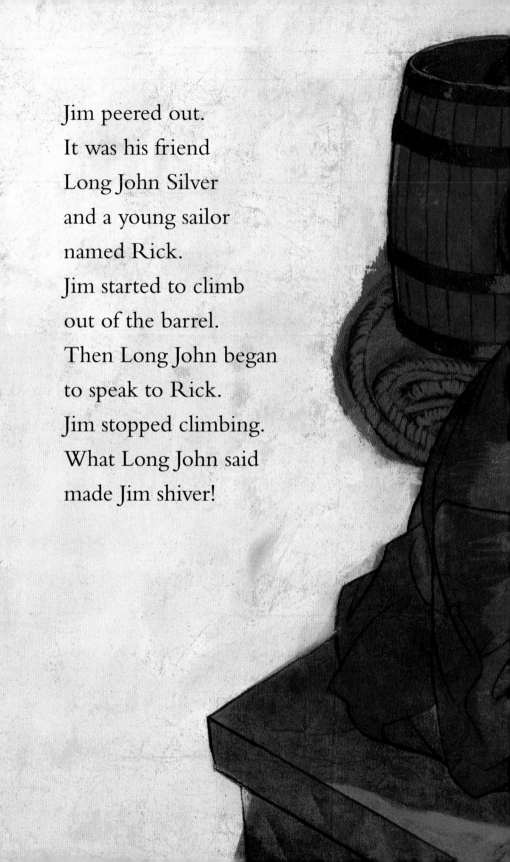

Jim peered out.
It was his friend
Long John Silver
and a young sailor
named Rick.
Jim started to climb
out of the barrel.
Then Long John began
to speak to Rick.
Jim stopped climbing.
What Long John said
made Jim shiver!

"I sailed with Flint,"
Long John said.
"What a pirate he was!"
Inside the barrel,
Jim listened closely.
If Long John Silver
had sailed with Flint,
Long John was a pirate, too!

"I heard Flint buried
all his treasure," said Rick.

"Yes," Long John said.
"He buried it where
this ship is headed—
on Treasure Island!"

Then Long John told Rick
there were other pirates
right on this very ship!
Long John was their leader.
He asked Rick to join them.
Right away, Rick said, "Yes!"

"Good!" said Long John.
"When we get there,
we will let the captain
and his friends
find the treasure.
Then we will steal it!"

Jim was very angry.
Long John was not
his friend at all!
He was planning
to steal the treasure!

"All this treasure talk
has made me hungry,"
Long John told Rick.
"Bring me an apple."
Rick jumped to his feet.

Jim's heart pounded.
What would happen
if they found him?
Then Jim heard a shout—
"Land ho! Land ho!"

Land had been spotted!
After Long John and Rick
rushed to the deck
with the rest of the sailors,
Jim climbed out of the barrel.

Jim joined the sailors.
In the distance was
Treasure Island!
Jim saw the captain.
Jim had to tell him
what he had heard.

The captain dropped his hat.
Jim picked it up.

"Here, sir," Jim said.
Then Jim whispered
that he needed to speak
with him in his cabin.

"Let's go, then,"
the captain said.

In the captain's cabin
were Jim's friends
Squire Trelawney
and Doctor Livesey.

"The boy here
has some news,"
said the captain.

"Speak up, then,"
the squire said.
So Jim told them
what he had heard.

When Jim finished,
there was silence.
Then the squire spoke.
  "Pirates on my ship?"
We must get rid of them!"

"There are more of them
than of us," said the doctor.

"We must wait," said the captain.

"Wait?" the squire said.
"How will we know
what they are up to?"

Jim stepped forward.

"I could watch them," he said.
"I am only a boy, after all.
They will not suspect me.
I can tell you their plans.
Then you can take action."
The men agreed to the idea.

"Welcome to the team, Jim,"
said the squire.

CHAPTER THREE

On the Island

Jim Hawkins was just a small boy,
but he had an important job.
He was a cabin boy
on a big ship.
The ship had sailed
for many days.
Now it had reached
Treasure Island.
Jim and his friends hoped
to find the treasure that
was buried there.

The ship's captain came on deck
with Jim's two friends.
There was Squire Trelawney,
who owned the ship,
and David Livesey, the ship's doctor.
All three men looked worried.
Pirates had hidden on the ship.
They wanted to steal the treasure.

"The pirates want to
take over the ship,"
said the captain.
"But their leader, Long John Silver,
has told them to wait.
He wants us to find
the treasure first."
"What will we do?" asked Jim.
"We have to get them off the ship,"
said the captain.
"And I know how."

He called to the crew.

"No more work!

You have the afternoon off.

Go and explore Treasure Island."

The men cheered.

The pirates got ready
to leave.
Jim watched them.
What would they do
on the island?
What trouble would
they cause?

Jim didn't stop
to think.
He stepped
into a boat.
He hid
under a sail.

He would go
to Treasure Island.
He would spy on the pirates
and report back
to the captain.
But one thing worried him.
Was he being very brave
or very foolish?

Jim was scared.
What if the pirates found him?
He walked deeper
into the woods.

What a strange island it was!
It was filled
with odd-looking trees,
plants, and creatures.
Jim felt like an explorer!

Then Jim heard a noise.

He turned quickly.

Who was there?

Someone was running
from tree to tree.
The creature was bent over.
Its arms almost touched
the ground.

Jim ran.

The creature ran, too!

It was coming after him!

Jim was running
toward the pirates.
Wait!
He didn't want
them to see him.
It would be safer
to face the creature!

Jim turned around.
"Who are you?"
he shouted.

The creature fell
on its knees
before Jim.
"I am Ben Gunn," he said.
The creature was a man!
But what a strange-looking man!
His hair was long.
His clothes were rags.
"How did you get here?" Jim asked.

"I came by ship," said Ben.

"I knew treasure was buried here.

My ship's crew came with me.

We looked and looked,

but we didn't find it.

"The crew was angry with me.

One day they left.

They didn't take me.

That was three years ago."

Jim gasped.

Three years was a long time.

No wonder Ben looked

the way he did!

"What do you eat?" Jim asked.

"I eat berries and goat meat," said Ben.

"But I dream of cheese.
Oh, how I would love
some cheese.
Do you have any?"

"No," said Jim.

"But there is cheese
on the ship."

"What ship?"
asked Ben.

So Jim told Ben
all his adventures.
He ended his story
with the pirates.
"They are on this island,"
said Jim.

Just then a cannon fired.
Sounds of fighting
filled the air.
Jim and Ben ran
deeper into the woods.
They hid in a cave.

At last the noise stopped.

It was safe to come out.

"My friends must have

left the ship to fight

the pirates," Jim said.

He wanted to see his friends.

He wanted to make sure

they were all right.

"Look!" said Ben.

Up ahead was a fort.

"Your friends are inside."

"How do you know?"

Jim asked.

Ben pointed to the flag.

It was from the ship.

"If the pirates had won,

they would be flying

their flag," he said.

"Come meet my friends,"
Jim said.
"Tomorrow," Ben said.
"Tonight I'll sleep in my cave.
I feel safer there.

But if you promise
to get me
off this island,
I'll help you
and your friends
fight the pirates.
You have my word."

Jim promised.
He said good–bye
to his new friend.
Then he hurried to the fort.
What adventures he was having!
And tomorrow he was sure
to have more!

CHAPTER FOUR

Pirate Attack

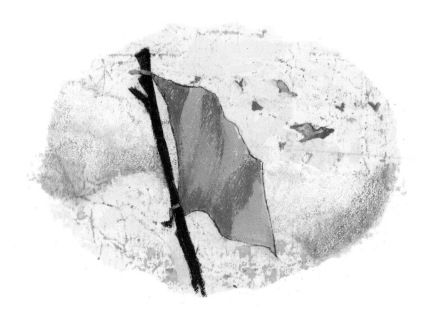

Jim Hawkins was a small boy
on a big adventure.
He had sailed with friends
to Treasure Island.
But pirates were
on the island, too!
The pirates wanted
the treasure buried there.
But first they needed the map
that Jim's friends had.

Luckily, Jim and his friends
found a fort
with a cabin.
It would help
keep them safe
from the pirates.

The morning after
finding the fort,
Jim awakened to the sound of voices.
He was the last one up!
Everyone else was busy working.
Suddenly, Jim heard a cry.
He ran outside.

The ship's captain
had spotted the leader
of the pirates—
Long John Silver!
"He's coming to the fort!"
the captain shouted.

Jim looked
through a hole
in the wall.

Long John was waving
a white flag.
That meant he
wanted to talk,
not fight.

The captain let Long John
come inside the fort.
"I have an offer to make,"
said Long John.
"What is it?"
asked the captain.

"I want the treasure map,"
said Long John.
"If you give it to me,
I'll take you to an island
where you will be safe."

Long John held out his hand.
"Is it a deal?" he asked.

"It is not," said the captain.

He did not shake the pirate's hand.

"But I have an offer
for you and the other pirates,"
the captain said. "Give yourselves up.
I will take you home.
You will have a fair trial.
I give you my word."

Long John threw
the white flag
on the sand.
"We will never give up!"
he said. "Soon you'll wish
you had taken my offer."

Jim watched Long John go.
The pirate was angry.
Next time, he would be back
to fight, not talk.

The captain had his men
line up at the wall.
That way they could
see the pirates
if they attacked the fort.

But the pirates were quick.
They rushed at the fort.
They climbed over the wall
like monkeys.

Now the pirates were
inside the fort!
They wanted
the treasure map!
Where was it?

Jim ran
into the fort's cabin.
The map was sticking out
of a jacket pocket.
Jim snatched it and ran.

Outside, there were pirates
everywhere.
One pirate was running
toward Jim!

Jim had no time to be afraid.
He jumped out of the way—
and slipped!

Down the hill Jim rolled!

At the bottom,
Jim got to his feet.
He wasn't hurt,
but where was the map?

Jim looked around.
There it was,
in the tall grass!
He ran over and picked it up.
Jim hid the map
inside a tree.
It would be safe there.
Then he went up the hill
to help his friends.

At the top of the fort
Jim let out a cheer.
"Hooray!" he cried.
The captain and his men
had won the battle.
The pirates were gone.

Jim's friends were
inside the cabin.
There was Squire Trelawney,
whose ship they had sailed on,
and David Livesey, a doctor.
Both men were upset.
The captain was trying
to calm them.

"What's wrong?" Jim asked.

"The pirates are gone,
and that is good."

"Yes," said the squire,
"but so is the map!"

"The pirates must have found it,"
said the doctor.

Jim didn't like to see
his friends upset, but he
couldn't stop laughing.
"What's so funny?"
asked the captain.

"I know where
the map is, sir," said Jim.
All three men stared at him.
Jim told them his story.
"So the map is safe," he said.
"I hid it in a tree."

The captain shook Jim's hand.
"That was quick thinking,
young man," he said.
"You are a hero."
Jim felt proud.
The map was safe.
The pirates would not
be back today.
For now, they were safe
on Treasure Island.

CHAPTER FIVE

Adventure at Sea

Jim Hawkins was trapped.
He and his friends had a map
that led to buried treasure.
But pirates were attacking their fort
on Treasure Island.
The pirates wanted the treasure, too.

The map was safe in the fort,
and so were Jim and his friends.
But for how long?

The pirates left the fort.
Some stayed on the island.
Others stole the ship that
Jim and his friends had sailed
to Treasure Island.

If the pirates got away,
Jim and his friends would be left behind.
Jim needed a plan—and fast!

What if Jim could somehow
get to the ship?
He could cut the rope
tied to the anchor.
The ship would drift to the shore
and get stuck in the sand.
Then the pirates couldn't sail away.

The plan was dangerous.
Jim's friends didn't want him to go.
Jim made up his mind.
He would go anyway.
He grabbed some snacks
for his dinner.
Then he took a sharp knife
to cut the rope.

Jim waited
until his friends were busy.
Then he slipped
out of the fort.
He ran into the woods.
He was free!

Jim walked down to the beach.
The ship looked
almost the same,
only now a pirate flag
was tied to its mast.
Seeing it made Jim angry.
How he wished
he could tear the flag down!

Jim knew where
he could find a boat.
A friend had hidden one
near a white rock.
Jim went to the spot.
There was the boat!
It was as round as a cup
and very small.

As soon as it grew dark,
Jim climbed into the boat.
He could just fit inside.
The night was foggy.
No one would see him.

At first, it was hard
to row the round boat,
but with practice,
he was able to steer it.
Soon he was beside
the tall ship.

A thick rope kept the ship
from sailing.
Jim began to cut the rope.
It was slow work.
Finally only a few strands
were left.

Jim slashed at the last pieces of rope.
As the rope dropped into the water,
the ship started to drift away.
Jim hoped it would get stuck in
the sand.

Just at that moment a strong wind blew.

The ship went faster.

So did Jim's boat.

Waves tossed it this way and that.

Jim rowed and rowed.

If he couldn't get back to shore,

he would be swept out to sea!

All night Jim's boat went
round and round Treasure Island.
No matter how hard he rowed,
he couldn't get close to shore.
Ahead of him, the big ship drifted, too.
No one was steering it.
The pirates must have jumped
off the ship in the storm.

Finally it was morning.
Jim was tired and thirsty.
His arms hurt from rowing.
He couldn't go on
for much longer.
What would happen to him?

Somehow he had to get
onto the ship.
Maybe he could steer it
back to shore.
Then his friends would have
their ship back.

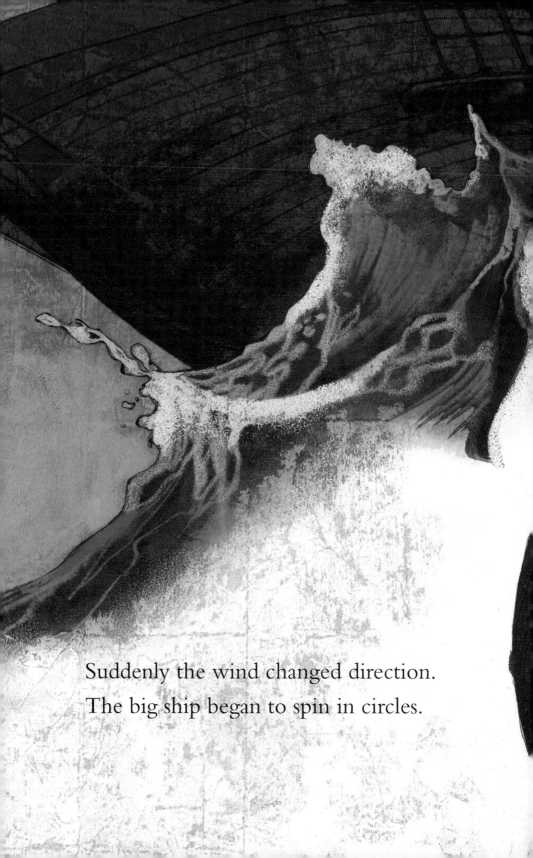

Suddenly the wind changed direction.
The big ship began to spin in circles.

When the wind stopped,
Jim saw that
the ship had turned around.
Now it was pointed at Jim.
And it was racing
toward his little boat!

A long pole stuck out
from the ship.
As it passed over him,
Jim reached up.
He grabbed it
with both hands.
He held on tight.

He was just in time.

The ship crashed into the boat.

The small boat sank without a trace.

Jim clung to the pole.

His feet dangled in the air.

Carefully, he pulled himself up.

At last his feet touched the deck.

Jim searched the ship
for pirates.
He was alone.
Suddenly he knew
what he had to do.

Jim climbed to the top of the mast.
He grabbed the pirate flag
and tore it down.
It fell on the deck below.
"I am captain of this ship," he shouted.

Jim made a new plan.
He would steer the ship
to a part of the island
where no one could find it.
Later he and his friends
would sail off and leave
the pirates behind.

In the distance
Jim saw the fort.
He couldn't wait
to see his friends again.
He had so much to tell them
about his adventure at sea!

CHAPTER SIX

A Pirate Adventure

Jim Hawkins walked swiftly
through the dark woods
of Treasure Island.
He was on his way
to see his friends
at a fort on the island.

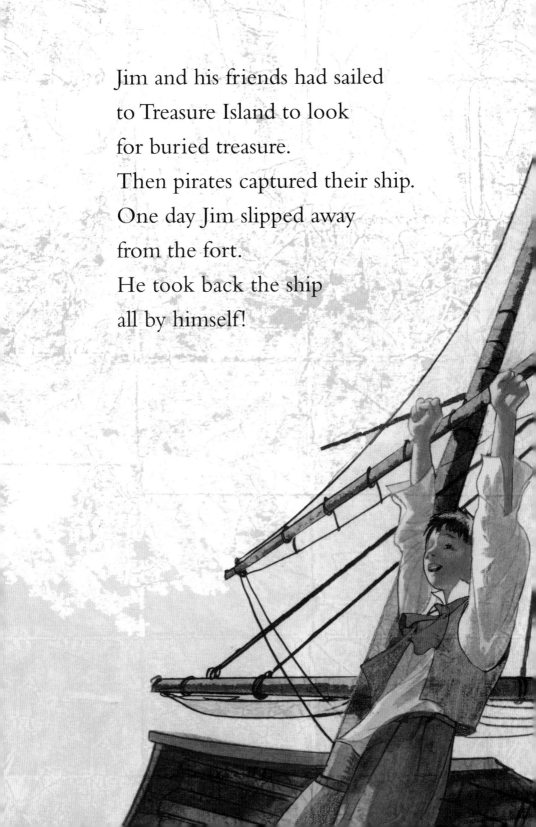

Jim and his friends had sailed
to Treasure Island to look
for buried treasure.
Then pirates captured their ship.
One day Jim slipped away
from the fort.
He took back the ship
all by himself!

Now Jim couldn't wait
to tell his friends
about his adventure at sea.
At last he came to the fort.
He climbed the fort's tall wall.

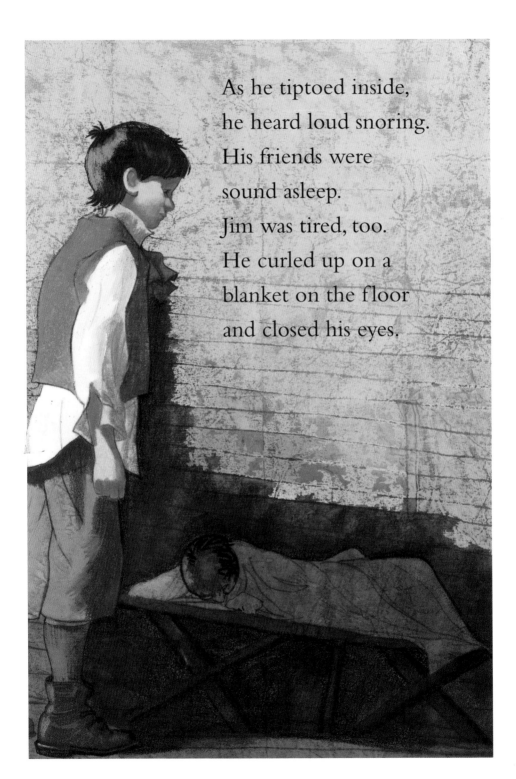

As he tiptoed inside,
he heard loud snoring.
His friends were
sound asleep.
Jim was tired, too.
He curled up on a
blanket on the floor
and closed his eyes.

"Squawk! Squawk!"
A loud noise filled the cabin.
Jim jumped to his feet.
He knew what that sound was.

It was a parrot.

None of his friends had a parrot,
but the leader of the pirates did.
His name was Long John Silver.

Just then, someone lit a torch.
Jim blinked.
He was surrounded by pirates!
Jim tried to break free.
He dashed for the door,
but someone grabbed him.

Long John Silver stood
in front of Jim.
His parrot sat on one shoulder.
"Look who it is!" Long John said.
"Jim Hawkins has stopped by
to visit us."

Jim did not see Doctor Livesey
or any of his other friends.

"Your friends are gone," Long John said.

"And they gave us this fort."

"They would never do that," Jim said.

"But they did," said Long John.

"Now you can join us."

"I will never be a pirate," Jim shouted.

"Never!"

Long John reached inside his coat pocket.
He took out an envelope.
"This might change your mind.
Look what your friends gave me."
He unfolded the paper inside.
It was the treasure map!

That night Jim could not sleep.

He had too many questions.

Where were his friends?

What had the pirates done to them?

And what would they do to *him*?

Jim tossed and turned all night.

Finally it was morning.
The pirates were ready
to look for the treasure.
"You're coming with us,"
Long John told Jim.
He tied a rope
around Jim's waist.
Now Jim couldn't escape.

The treasure was at the top of a hill.
As they climbed, Jim kept falling.
Each time, Long John yanked
on the rope and pulled
him up.

At last they reached the top.
Long John pointed to
a large X on the map.
"The treasure is near
the tallest tree," he said.
One pirate ran up ahead.
Then he gave a shout.

All the pirates ran.

Jim ran, too.

They stopped at a
giant hole in the ground.

"Someone got to the treasure first!"
Long John shouted.

Some of the pirates jumped
into the hole.
They dug at the dirt with their hands.
One pirate held up a coin.
"We came all this way for this?"
he shouted.

The pirates were angry.
They thought Long John
had tricked them.
Jim was afraid.
What would they do now?

Just then Jim heard a scary voice.

"Bring me my sword," it said.

"Who is that?" a pirate asked.

"I know that voice,"
said Long John.

"It belongs to a pirate
by the name of Flint."

Jim knew that Flint
had buried the treasure.
He had died long, long ago.
"Flint has come back,"
Long John said.
"He wants his treasure."
The pirates began to shiver.
Their faces were white with fear.

Long John let go of the rope
around Jim's waist.

"Let's go!" he shouted.

"I don't want to see Flint's ghost!"

All the pirates ran down the hill.

Jim didn't want to go
with the pirates.
But he didn't want to
be alone either—
not with a ghost around.

Then Jim heard laughing.
There was Doctor Livesey!
His friend Ben Gunn
was there, too.
Jim waved to them.

"I tricked them," Ben said.

"Those pirates thought I was a ghost!"

"Was that you, Ben?" Jim asked.

"You sounded so spooky!"

"Yes, it was," said Ben.

"It was old Ben Gunn."

"Our treasure is safe now,"

the doctor said.

Jim pointed at the hole.

"No, it's not," he told his friends.

"Someone has dug it up."

His friends laughed.

"Yes," said Ben.

"I did!"

Jim told his friends
about his adventure at sea.
"Thank you," the doctor said.
"You helped us get back our ship."

He gave Jim a gold coin.

"This is for you," he said.

"And there's much more to come."

Jim was happy.
They had found the treasure,
and he and his friends were safe.
Now, after all that had happened
on Treasure Island,
he was even happier
to be going home!